Windy Meadows

Mares and foals

Entrance

The Tails of Windy Meadows

Ellen Troutman

Illustrated by: Debra K. Leet

ISBN 978-1-935497-09-7
Printed in Canada
Manufactured by Friesens Corporation
Manufactured in Altona, MB, Canada in October 2009
Job # 118264

Illustrations by Debra K. Leet

Book design by Scott Stortz

Published by:

Butler Books
P.O. Box 7311
Louisville, KY 40207
(502) 897-9393
Fax (502) 897-9797
www.butlerbooks.com

The Tails of Windy Meadows

Ellen Troutman

My most heartfelt thank you to my family, for their love, support and inspiration.

To the Windy Meadows family, for their commitment, dedication and understanding.

To my creative team and to Debra Leet, for her amazing illustrations and kindness.

To Leslie Moise, for believing in my dream and for her help in making it great.

To my mother, thanks for the best idea ever!

And to Windy Meadows, truly a special place for horses, dogs, kids and grown–ups.

Welcome to Windy Meadows, a real working horse farm outside LaGrange, Kentucky, located in an equestrian community called L'Esprit on Bluegrass Parkway. Bluegrass Parkway sounds like a long road or even a highway, doesn't it? But when you drive from one end to the other you have only traveled three miles. Although it is not a lengthy road, it is home to a very large horse population.

At the beginning of Bluegrass Parkway is a rehabilitation farm. Equipped with treadmills, a swimming pool and caring people, this place helps horses recover from injury or illness. Drive a little further and you will see the white oval racetrack nearly hidden in the thick pine trees. If you are lucky you may see a future Kentucky Derby contender breezing by.

Continue your journey by small farms, pastures full of horses, large houses and fields of hay. Now look up. Do you see it? There upon the hill? A massive smoke gray barn with chocolate trim appears to be rising up out of the hill. The sun reflects off the many windows. It is so beautiful.

Slow down and look closer. There is not just one barn, there are five.

Slowly now, it is nearly time to make your turn into the driveway.

Blue and gray Windy Meadows signs on each side of the entrance tell
you that you have found your way. Go through the tall stone pillars
that hold two black iron gates, up the paved driveway. Look to the
right at a small stand of trees and brush, home to our woodland
friends.

You may see a bunny making his way or a squirrel gathering acorns.
Why, just yesterday there was a doe munching some clover. Small
pine trees and large ornate street lamps line the driveway's left side.
A four–board oak fence painted black surrounds the pastures and
paddocks.

We are glad you are here!

Welcome to Windy Meadows.

Welcome to Windy Meadows!

So now you know this is a real place.

You also know where to find us.

Now I want to share with you

The Tails of Windy Meadows.

Turn the page and meet the heroes of our story.

The day starts early at Windy Meadows, even before the sun has come up. The silence is broken by the sound of the front gates slowly swinging open, allowing George's car to pass through. In the number 18 stall, Matem – the always curious and sometimes silly red chestnut – opens one sleepy eye.

He hears the car tires coming up the paved driveway. He shakes the sleep from his eyes, steps forward with both front feet and leans in for a deep stretch, while letting out a giant yawn.

I hope it's breakfast time. I am hungry.

The car tires turn onto the gravel parking lot. Soon, footsteps can be heard approaching the big double doors that separate in the middle and a tall dark–haired figure appears in the doorway.

After years of the aisle lights coming on at 5 o'clock in the morning, Matem knows George has come to clean the stalls. However, it does not stop him from letting out a low throaty nicker.

Good morning, George!

When George does not respond, Matem calls out a little louder.

Hey, George, how about a little snack? Just to hold me over until the breakfast cart gets here, or maybe just some HAY, George, adding a little snicker.

Matem loves a good horse joke!

SHHH, Matem, you'll wake the entire barn if you're not quiet. It will be an hour–and–a–half before breakfast. A small mouse voice whispers from behind Matem's feeder.

Hey, mouse, any stray kernels of corn you find under there belong to the owner of that feeder and that owner is ME!

George slides open stall 18's door only to find Matem already occupying the entrance.

"Buenos dias, Amigo." George smiles, as he gives Matem a hearty pat on the neck. Matem turns to examine George's hands and pockets for even the smallest of treats. No such luck. Just a muck tub and pitchfork.

No carrots? No apples? I'd settle for a piece of candy, a sugar cube, a cough drop...anything.

15

Turning to the window, Matem lets out a disappointed sigh. Tiny sunbeams stream into the window, landing on Matem's blazed face. The warmth causes his eyes to grow heavy. Voices float across the valley. The racetrack is bustling with activity. Shouts, whistles and thundering hoofs sound so close. The sun rays grow larger, the heat more intense, like the spotlights of the National Coliseum. Matem's mind drifts back to his show career and his sparkly maroon and gold native costume. These are his very favorite memories.

The music grows louder. Spotlights dance. Wind rushes into my flared nostrils. Fast at the canter. My tail is floating clear off the ground, and then faster to the gallop. My velvet costume billowing, gold tassels flowing and spinning, adorned with beads and crystals. Horses to my left and horses to my right. You won't pass me. I charge up through my bridle, the bit in my teeth. A true Bedouin's delight. The music slows and the lights dim, telling us it's time to line up for inspection.

"Head to tail," the announcer calls out, so everyone watching can see the magnificent costumes and the judges can compare each one.

I've got my place in line. I keep shifting my weight back and forth, resting a back foot, anything to keep from being so nervous. My feet just won't stand still. My heart is racing wildly. I've got to know. Did I win?

"Matem." "Matem."

"Good morning, Matem. Horse showing in your dreams again? It must have been good. You were sound asleep. I had to call you twice," smiles Miss Ellie, adjusting her blonde pony tail and pulling her Windy Meadows ball cap down. "No horse I know loved to show as much as you did. Maybe one day we'll take you out to show for old time's sake, what do you say, ol' boy?"

Oh rats! Just a dream. A good dream, though.

Stretching his long neck and peeking over the stall wall, it's confirmed, the feed cart has arrived. Stepping back, Matem shakes his whole body, sending up a cloud of loose hair and pine shavings.

It's the feed cart with breakfast! Breakfast...breakfast! trumpets Matem, trotting in a circle.

"Easy, Matem, let me put your hay in the manger. Manners, please! Do not grab the hay." Miss Ellie thrusts her shoulder forward, placing herself between Matem and his feeder.

Hay, I love hay. Glorious, fragrant hay, yummy alfalfa.

The light tap of the metal feed door as it's latched reminds Matem he's just received his portion of grain.

Oh, more food! He gathers a mouthful.

Breakfast...the most important meal of the day!

Every meal is the most important one of the day for you. It's not so exciting when you're on a special diet, grumbles Sneaky Pete, also a bright red chestnut with a large white blaze, but far more serious then Matem.

Once again the metal tap. Feed pours into stall 19's feeder. Instead of the rain of oats and corn, it's more like the splat of a bucket full of plain oatmeal.

Soaked beet pulp... yuck! frowns Sneaky Pete.

0–700 hours...Breakfast cart fuel for the guts...On your feet, soldiers!
The tall, handsome and very athletic palomino calls orders from
stall 21.

*Hey Charley, we are on our feet. We're horses. We sleep standing
up, remember?* Sneaky Pete shakes his head, sending his long red
forelock to either side of his wide forehead.

No time to waste. Anyone ready for a workout? I'm starting mine now.
Long strands of blonde mane bouncing about, Charley starts a few
horse–style jumping jacks, some cardio running in place, a little yoga
balancing on hind legs, then standing on his front feet.

CHARLEY

Whoa! Whoa! I'm losing my balance. **POW!** *Exercising too close to the wall. Darn, I kicked the front of the stall again. Miss Ellie won't be very happy. She says I am impatient for my food and that my behavior is a bad example to the colts, but she just doesn't get it. I'm trying to start my workout. It just happens to be at feeding time and, of course, I wouldn't want to be skipped. Oh, no, it's too late!*

A chain reaction of whinnies, kicking and bucking sends the last aisle of unfed horses into a frenzy.

"Stop it, stop it right now." Miss Ellie appears from around the corner, sternly pointing to Charley. "Mister, you need to settle down."

How does she always know it's me? Looking puzzled, Charley steps to the window.

Maybe it's the giant dust cloud, circling around your head that gave it away. Twist bends, rubbing the corners of his big dark eyes on his knee.

"You are a seasoned show horse and need to set a good example for this entire barn," Miss Ellie tells Charley. "You know bad behavior only slows the feed cart. I could be feeding you instead of scolding you."

"They sure are rowdy this morning, aren't they, George?" George nods and smiles as Miss Ellie pushes the feed cart.

"Good morning, Princess." Pouring her grain, closing one door quickly, opening the next, zig–zagging back and forth across the wide aisle, Miss Ellie makes her way through the entire barn. The feeding and greeting continue down the aisle until every horse has received its own portion of hay and grain. The only sound that is heard now is of content horses crunching and munching and the splashing of water as each horse's water bucket is dumped and refilled.

The outside mares with their foals run to the gate and whinny to Miss Ellie.

Feed us. Feed us, too!

The feed cart exits the barn and heads outside to the awaiting herd.

Several cars make their way into the barn parking lot.

It's Jenny and Meg, the horse trainers. I love these girls. I am glad I have stall number 10 because I can see everyone from here, squeals Guess Who, a small stocky bay pony, with a large white backward question mark for a facial marking.

"Good morning, handsome." Tall and strong Meg runs her fingers across the metal bars of the front of the stall, as if she's waving.

Guess Who spins around on his hind legs in excitement.

I hope I am on today's schedule. Oh it's starting to get busy. I love busy. It's so exciting! Busy, busy, busy.

Guess Who races around his stall, charging up to the walls with excitement.

One more car rolls into the gravel parking lot. Ms. Pam, the farm manager, arrives with her car loaded from her morning errands. Using the rear-view mirror, she adjusts her hair band and pushes her wire-rimmed glasses back in place with her index finger. Ernie, one of the Windy Meadows dogs, a short-legged pudgy Pembroke Corgi, patiently waits for Ms. Pam to organize the car's contents and open the door.

"Why hello, Ernie. It is easier to pet you while I am closer to the ground," Ms. Pam chuckles, as she fumbles through her backpack, hoping to find a dog biscuit. To Ernie's delight, one is located.

"Here." Ernie gently removes the gift from Ms. Pam's fingers and flops down in the damp grass to enjoy the treat.

Ms. Pam makes her way into the barn, arms overflowing with mail, bagged carrots, a freshly–washed horse blanket and a thermos of coffee. Miss Ellie steps from the office, drying her hands, and discards a wrinkled paper towel.

"Good morning, ladies." Miss Ellie turns to Jenny and Meg, who have started preparing for the day's work by readying their grooming stations. Gathering brushes, hoof picks, supplies and tack, they are nearly ready to retrieve the first horses of the day.

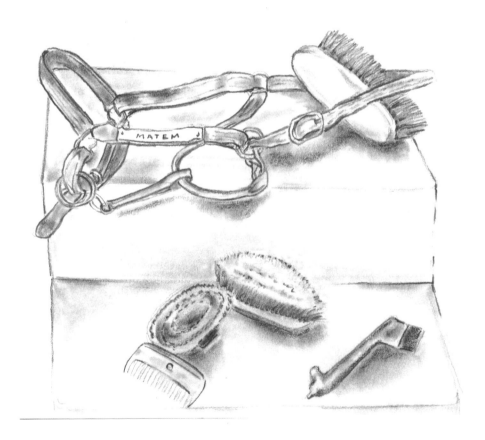

"I have put up the schedule board with the names of horses for you to work and groom today," Miss Ellie continues. The moment is interrupted by the thundering stampede of running, barking dogs on their way to greet Ms. Pam, whose load shifts and spills over onto the barn floor as she gets halfway down the aisle.

"Oh, hey, let me give you a hand with that," Jenny calls out, tossing a brush back into the grooming caddy.

"One of those mornings? Going to the office with this?" Jenny says, gathering up the blanket and its long straps. "I'll take it for you."

"We have a full day of grooming, exercising and training horses," says Miss Ellie. If anyone has any questions or needs help, let me know. Pam, let's check those mare lists to see when the babies are due. Jenny, you get Charley and put him in grooming station number 1. Meg, you start with Matem. He'll go in the number 2 grooming station. All right, let's get started. I'll get Twist, and Pam, when you get caught up, bring up the new horse from stall 22."

Here comes Miss Ellie. Beauty treatment time! Yeah, hoof shine, tail conditioner, mane tamer. Give me the works, my lady!

Slipping the brown leather halter over Twist's silky gray head and resting it just behind his ears, with a hand on each side of his face, Miss Ellie leans close.

"You do know you are the most beautiful horse on this farm, Twist?" She plants a kiss on his well–chiseled cheek.

World, you mean world! I'm the most beautiful horse in the world. Are you forgetting all my halter championships? Those are beauty contests. You must be beautiful to win.

Twist returns the peck on the cheek with a big sloppy lick.

"Wow, thanks, Twist." Wiping her face with her shirt sleeve and gathering up her lead line, Miss Ellie pokes her head outside the stall door to make sure the aisle is clear.

Jogging alongside Miss Ellie, Twist can hardly wait to be backed into his grooming station. A long stretchy tie hangs on each side of the stall toward the front. A wall divides each horse. Lockers at the back of each grooming station hold equipment. There are black rubber mats and a long metal drain on the floor. It is the perfect place for the horses to visit while receiving their grooming. The cross ties are securely fastened to each side of Twist's halter, leaving Miss Ellie's hands free to start brushing.

TWIST

Let's skip the foo foo grooming stuff, Charley says, as Jenny carefully backs him into grooming station number 1.

Knock the dirt off, slap the leather on and let's get to work. Charley stomps his hoof on the spongy mat.

A horse should receive a proper grooming before and after he's ridden, sniffs Twist. He turns his nose up and readjusts his recently combed salt-and-pepper-colored mane.

Personally, I would prefer just to skip the whole work thing anyway. Who wants to get all sweaty? I'll just stay in the grooming stall. Twist tosses his head up-and-down, in rhythm with Miss Ellie's brushing.

Wow, the stiff bristled brush feels the best.

It's a balance between grooming and hard work. That's what makes a great show horse. Matem leans into the conversation. *It's important.* Matem pauses and pulls forward, stretching the cross ties to stare down the aisle.

What is it, Matem? I can't see a thing from down here. Charley raises his head over the divided wall.

It's probably a single kernel of corn being hauled away from under Matem's feeder by that mouse, snorts Twist.

Real funny, Twist. I tell the jokes around here. It's a new horse. Ms. Pam's leading a new horse, and they're coming this way.

The stall mouse scurries up the tall post between Twist and Matem. *That's Bravo. He's new. Miss Ellie brought him back from the last show.*

Wait a minute, mouse. What did you say? Twist squints an eye and turns his head so he can get a good look at the mouse. *Whoa, someone left him at a show?* Twist stammers. *I told you something scary could happen. Did you all hear that? Someone forgot to load him. GREAT! Something else to worry about.* He nervously wrings his silver tail.

Maybe next time I'll simply refuse to go. Lock and no load. Yep that's what I am going to do.

Twist, get a hold of yourself, orders Charley. *Matem, what else can you see? Give us the details, man!*

Big...yeah, big. He's flashy...a pinto...two colors. No, a tri-color...Three colors. Matem strains to look. *He's coming this way. He must be sixteen hands. I bet he's a ground-pounding, earth-shaking heart-stopping English horse. How exciting!* Matem wiggles in place.

The impressive pinto is easily backed into the fourth grooming station and snapped into place by Ms. Pam.

Show horse. I'm sure he's a show horse. Just look at him! Matem shakes the dust and loose hair from his face after his brushing.

Hey, Matem, let's get the story from the horse himself, suggests Charley.

Don't you mean let's get the story straight from the horse's mouth? That's funny, you guys, a horse joke, Matem snorts.

Matem! Cool it, warns Charley, laying back his ears.

Hey, new horse, did you hear this one? Why did the pony go to the doctor? You don't know, do ya? Because he was a little horse. I love that one, whinnies Matem.

Matem, no one wants to hear your jokes, smirks Charley, trying to contain a laugh. *Now let the horse tell his own story. What's your name, soldier? I'm Charley.*

My name is Bravo, I was not left. I was bought at the show. My owner put up a sign that had my picture on it and the words "FOR SALE." He promised me a good home. I was raised on a South Carolina horse farm near the ocean.

Ocean? interrupts Matem, as he pricks his ears up. *Are there show horses in the ocean?* He turns his head to one side and raises an eyebrow.

There's going to be a short, stocky costume horse in the ocean if you don't button your lip! Charley lifts one hind leg as a warning. *Go on, Bravo.*

Thanks, Charley. As I was saying, life was good, but when it was time to start my training, they had it all wrong. Everyone was sure I would follow in the hoof prints of my English Champion parents. But I dreamed of belonging to a cowboy. Big Western saddle dripping in silver, a Navajo style wool pad, leather chaps, cowboy hats, spurs. Well, maybe not spurs. Long story short, Miss Ellie bought me for Mr. Randy, her husband. I am his new cowboy horse.

Welcome to Windy Meadows, soldier. Show name–Eighteen Carats. Of course, you know my barn name–Charley. Discipline–Western Pleasure. Division–Youth. Kids' horse. Most important job around here. I'm on the A–string. That means I'm the first on the trailer every time. Yes, sir!

Well, first to go when you're not on the injured reserve list, reminds Twist.

*Thanks for the reminder, Twist. This...*lifting his right foot up...*is a battle scar. Got it in the line of duty.*

Battle scar? Twist looks puzzled. *Charley has a metal plate with four screws drilled into his hoof wall, holding together a big split called a quarter crack.*

Oh, hey, there's my saddle. Love the smell of leather. Charley breathes deeply. *Thanks, Jenny!*

Me too, inhales Bravo. *I've been waiting all my life to carry my cowboy saddle. I wear it with pride, that's for sure.*

Me, personally, I think that saddle stinks like too much work. I like the smell of rose water shampoo and lavender conditioner. Twist stretches out a foreleg, looking at his freshly–polished hoofs.

"Hey, Jenny," says Miss Ellie. "Give Charley a light workout. Just walk and jog only."

"Okay, Miss Ellie." Jenny lifts the bit to Charley's mouth, placing the bridle over one ear and then the other before heading out to the covered arena.

We're right behind you, Charley, hollers Matem, tail raised in the air like a flag and trotting in place.

"Slow down, Matem. Let me get my gloves. Slow down! I can't get my helmet fastened. What's your hurry?" Meg tucks her brown bangs behind her ears.

I've got my lucky saddle on and Meg always gives me an apple if I'm good.

"No saddle for you today, Twist, just a little exercise on the long line. Pam, do you mind giving him about fifteen minutes on the line?" Miss Ellie hands her the lead. "I'm going to hop on Bravo and see what he knows."

"I don't mind at all." Ms. Pam reaches for the long blue line and snaps the brass chain to the bottom ring on Twist's halter.

With a foot in the left stirrup and two quick hops, Miss Ellie is atop Bravo. "I'm headed outside for a farm ride." Miss Ellie's voice fades as she rides down the long aisle.

"Hey, Guess Who, you're on Tayler's list. She'll ride you after school." Miss Ellie continues through the open doors and onto the driveway.

Guess Who looks forward to his girl, Tayler, getting home from school and giving him his workout.

I can hardly wait for Tayler. I wonder how long it will be. Maybe I'll take a little snooze before she arrives. I should rest. She likes to go fast, and so do I. Guess Who makes several circles before folding his legs and dropping to the ground. He closes his eyes and quickly opens them.

What is that? Something is staring at me through the cracks between the boards. Big dark lashes and knobby knees...that's all I can make out. What is that thing?

I'm not a what. I'm a who. The tiniest of horse voices comes through the cracks between the oak stall boards.

Guess Who stands up to get a better look. *Oh, wow, a baby.*

You mean a foal. I'm a foal, not a baby. A filly to be exact, the voice returns.

Great, that's what this place needs. Another sassy girl horse. I'd better get back to my nap.

Wait a minute, young man. A mare's voice comes from the same stall. It's the kindest, softest, most beautiful voice Guess Who has ever heard. He turns around to see a face that matches the voice. Huge, dark, sparkly eyes with long curly eyelashes stare back at him.

My name is Princess, the mare says gently. She leans down to nuzzle her foal, who flips her bushy tail and scurries behind her mother.

Of course it is. What other name could she have? Guess Who swishes his long black tail.

Allow me to introduce you to my filly, Aurora. Princess nuzzles the curly-coated brown foal, who is staggering toward Guess Who's wall. *Don't push me, Momma.* Aurora bounces up a little baby buck.

Welcome to Windy Meadows, Aurora. It is a very special place, nods Guess Who.

What's so special about it? asks the foal.

Well, that depends on who you ask. Guess Who moves closer to the bars. *It's different for each horse or pony. Everyone has a story here, just ask them.*

Do you have a story, Mr. Guess Who? asks Aurora.

I have a great story, but it's super long. We'll save that for a rainy day. I bet your mom has a great story. Let's see if she'll tell it.

Princess, how about your story? Guess Who perks his ears up.

Of course. I had an owner who was very busy and we rarely spent time together. It made him sad because I was lonely. He sent me on a long trailer ride to Windy Meadows, hoping that Miss Ellie would find me a forever home.

One day, Mr. Randy walked down the barn aisle and I thought he was my owner. I was able to get his attention, only to find out I didn't know him at all. But he seemed to really like me, and I instantly liked him too. He was already in my stall, rubbing my face, when Miss Ellie rounded the corner.

"That's the mare from New Jersey. She's here to be sold."

Everyday he would come to my stall, sometimes bringing me an apple or a carrot, or sometimes just to talk. I loved the attention. And then one morning Mr. Randy called Miss Ellie to my stall.

"I think we should keep Princess."

"Here's the problem. She should be a broodmare, having foals. We train horses, show horses, and give lessons. We don't raise foals," Miss Ellie said, very matter-of-fact.

"I say we buy Princess, give her a forever home raising foals here at Windy Meadows."

And that's exactly what happened. I have two babies that are growing up to be show horses and I have Aurora. Windy Meadows is a special place for me to have my very own person, Mr. Randy, and to raise my fillies.

Princess turns to find her filly curled up in the corner fast asleep.

Outside, Guess Who hears the sound of hoofs on gravel. It's Miss Ellie, returning from her farm ride. She stops Bravo at the gate at the end of the covered arena to watch the horses work. "Matem looks good, Meg. How's Charley doing, Jeremy?"

"Looks like he wants to do more than walk and jog." Miss Ellie smiles and shakes her head.

Jenny smiles back, "He's been a little anxious, but he's working okay."

"I think we're about ready for lunch. Let's get these horses cooled out and put away." Miss Ellie rides on in, dismounts and begins unlacing the saddle straps. Jenny dismounts from Charley.

We can't be finished yet. I'm just getting warmed up! Where's my girl, Tayler? She'd take me outside. She'd let me run.

She's in school. Hey, maybe Miss Ellie would let us barn–school Tayler. Matem turns his ear sideways. *I think I just heard Miss Ellie call lunch.*

What a workout, Matem said, nearly dragging Meg back to the barn aisle.

"Lunch time!" Ms. Pam brings the loaded cart down the main aisle on her way to the mares and foals.

Oh, goody, after my grooming and a great workout, I could use a lunch break. What's on the menu? whinnies Matem.

No lunch for you, Matem. Just the mommas and babies, Ernie replies.

Wait a minute. Those big lazy cows? They haven't missed a meal in fifteen show seasons. Matem swishes his tail.

Listen here, you little tassel-wearing, sequin-sewing costume gypsy, Spicey squeals, pinning her ears and diving at Matem.

Whoa! Help! Someone help! Where did she come from? Matem flies backward in the cross ties.

Let me tell you, sometimes I have three babies by my side and one on the way. Furthermore, you call us cows again and I'll kick you to your next horse show!

Move along, Spicey. Matem's just trying to be funny. I emphasize trying! Ernie weaves back and forth behind the ankles of Spicey and her three foals.

Keep moving, gals. Lunch is waiting. Ernie keeps herding.

Hey, Ernie!

Yes, Matem.

Any of those foals look like a costume prospect? I'm all about training the next champion. Matem straightens up trying to appear taller and slimmer.

Matem, if you want to help with the foals, you'd better be nicer to the mares.

You need to be positive, Ernie reminds Matem.

I am positive, Ernie. I am positive I need lunch and they don't!

Twist pushes his nostrils through the bars of his door.

Ernie, Spicey seemed a little short-tempered today. What's going on?

Well, Twist, another mare gave up her foal last night, Ernie replies, shaking his head. *I don't understand it. This makes three Spicey's caring for. She sure is an amazing mare. But that's a story for a rainy day. I'll finish later. I gotta run. The Jack Russell has the mouse cornered. I need to help.*

I thought you said positive, Ernie. Catching and killing mice isn't very positive, Matem smirks.

Oh, you think I'm going to help Jack? You've got it all wrong. I have an agreement with the mice. I go to assist the Russell, or so he thinks. I get in the way and give the mouse a chance to escape.

Wow! An apple. Hey! An apple just landed in my feeder. Yeah, a treat. I love treats. Hurry! Get me back to my stall. Matem pulls Meg toward his stall. She unbuckles his halter and he pulls away and runs to his feeder.

Why does Matem always get apples? Sneaky Pete looks puzzled, as he's led through the small outside door into the barn and to his stall.

Because I am a star. A celebrity. People want to honor me with gifts. Matem drools apple juice, tossing his head around.

No, it's because people want him to shut up, and if he has food in his mouth, he isn't going on about horse shows and costumes.

You've got that right, Charley...Oh, no way, I got an apple too, pipes up Sneaky Pete, almost letting go of a smile.

Me, too. I got one. Charley proudly marches over to his feeder.

"Hi, Tayler." Jenny gives a wave.

"Hey, Jenny, how are you?"

Hey, Tayler? Matem butts in, striking the front of his stall with his horseshoe.

"Hey, sweet boy, no striking. Looks like you've been worked already today. Would you like a carrot?" Ducking into the office, right next to Matem's stall, she reappears with a handful of carrots.

For me? Matem's eyes bulge.

"Listen, you can't tell the others I gave you all this." She opens his feed door and drops them in.

OH MY GOSH, look at all these carrots Tayler just gave me! I told you guys she loves me best!

"Matem, you silly horse, now everyone knows our carrot secret."

Tayler laughs and returns to the office, retrieving a giant armload of carrots and apples. "A little something for each of my very special horse friends. One for you, Charley."

See, Matem, I got one too. Charley tosses his golden mane.

"Twist, my silver steed, here's your treat." Tayler rests an apple between the stall bars, letting him eat from her hand.

Ha! my apple was fed by hand.

"Pete," Tayler whispers, "Here are two carrots, better than that sloppy diet food." She winks, putting the goodies into the feeder without a sound.

Hello, I'm waiting here in the cross ties. I need to be saddled. Guess Who stands on his hind legs, too small to see down the aisle. *Horses aren't supposed to be left unattended. Hello?*

"I'm on my way. Sorry, I got carried away with the treats." Tayler unlocks the tack room, gets her saddle, a bridle and Guess Who's bell boots and returns to the grooming station.

"Let me help you with your saddle." Jenny lifts the small English saddle and places it on Guess Who's back. "Let me put these bell boots on him and then I'm ready to ride. I'll need you to hold him while I get on. He's always a little wild."

Wild? Guess Who flashes a confused look. *You mean jazzed, ready to ROAD GAIT. Let's go!*

What's a road gait? Twist wrinkles his nose. *That Guess Who is a lively little guy! He makes me a little nervous.*

Road gait is part of his show routine. It's a super fast trot, Matem chimes in, still munching carrots.

The pounding sound of horse hoofs catches Twist's attention. *Where are you going, guys?* Twist strolls to the front of his stall.

We have to give riding lessons. You should join us, Twist. Sneaky Pete struts across the aisle for his turn in the grooming stations.

Yeah, I get to ride two times today. Bravo returns to the grooming station next to Sneaky Pete.

Miss Ellie brings out two very small saddles, one for each horse. "Miss Pam, will you help me get the lesson horses ready?"

"Sure, no problem. She tosses a red woven pad onto Bravo's back, followed by one of the small leather western saddles. Pam adjusts the stirrups to fit the small riders.

Miss Ellie saddles Sneaky Pete and leads him and Bravo to the covered arena. The students wait eagerly for their turn to ride.

"Helmets, boots and smiles...looks like you're ready to ride. Callie, you get Bravo." Miss Ellie stops the big pinto next to the eager red head.

"Jana, you'll be riding Sneaky Pete." Miss Ellie hands her the reins. "Tayler will be riding Guess Who for her lesson. He is much faster. You will need to stay on the rail. I will help each of you girls get on." Miss Ellie cups her hand and stoops, making an easy step for the rider.

"Jana and Callie, move to the jog. Tayler, step up to a strong trot." Miss Ellie walks a circle, her head slightly turned to watch all three riders.

Look out, lesson horses. You're about to get a face full of dirt and tail! Guess Who looks back, as he swiftly paces.

Sneaky Pete continues his steady stride. *We tell you every time, we like going slow, and we don't care if you pass us.*

Almost time for road gait! I'll be so fast you won't even see me. Guess Who zooms by. *Passed you again.*

He just doesn't get it, does he? Bravo laughs.

"Okay, Tayler, let him go, road gait." Miss Ellie waves them on. Tayler's kiss sound sends Guess Who into his third gear. His knees snap high. The pair make three laps at lightning speed.

"Whoa, Guess Who, time to come back to the walk." Tayler pulls back on the reins and slows the excited pony.

Guess Who skips a few extra steps. *Yahoo, that was great!*

"Everyone, walk now." Miss Ellie checks her watch. "Just a few more rounds and it will be time to dismount."

"I'll help you un–tack the lesson horses." Jenny enters the arena, with Jack and Ernie following at her heels.

Miss Ellie extends her arms, signaling the young riders to stop in front of her. "Bring the lesson horses to the middle, girls."

The horses and their girls line up side–by–side.

"I love Bravo, he is such a great horse." Callie wraps her arms around Bravo's neck and gives him a squeeze.

I love you too! Bravo turns his head to nuzzle Callie's brown paddock boot.

"Sneaky Pete was really good. He makes me so happy, I can't wait until my next lesson." Jana scratches Sneaky Pete's shoulders. He shakes his head up and down with the scratching.

I am happy too! Sneaky Pete agrees.

The long parade of riders, horses, dogs and trainers makes its way back into the barn.

"Everyone, remove the saddles and give each horse a good brushing, please. I shouldn't see any saddle marks." Miss Ellie points to the sweaty hair left by the saddle blanket.

Jenny returns the two lesson saddles to the tack room across the aisle. "I'll help you with Buck when you are finished with Guess Who, Tayler."

"Thanks, Jenny. I'm looking forward to giving Buck his very first ride." Tayler's blue eyes sparkle with excitement.

Jenny leads the small buttermilk–colored colt with the black mane and tail to the round pen at the end of the arena. "Tayler, we're ready." Jenny calls to her in the barn.

"Just a second, let me get a treat for Guess Who. He was awesome today." Tayler pulls a peppermint from her pocket.

A peppermint! My favorite treat ever! Tayler unwraps the mint. *The crinkle sound! Gimme, gimme.* Guess Who darts at Tayler like a snake.

Jenny leads Buck in a small circle. She stops to put her weight in the stirrup to check his reaction and then continues the circles.

Callie, Jana and Tayler walk side–by–side to the arena gates, giggling and smiling.

"Be careful." Callie pats Tayler's back.

"I like Buck, he's really cute." Jana smiles without her two front teeth.

A horn honks in the parking lot. "Our mom's here. We wanted to watch, but we have to go." The girls turn and head to the parking lot.

"Bye, Tayler! Bye, Jenny! Bye, Miss Ellie!" The goodbyes fade as they run to the car.

Tayler snaps the shiny helmet under her chin as she makes her way to the round pen.

"Are you ready, Tayler?" Jenny flashes a big smile.

"I'm a little nervous, but excited" She rubs her hands together anxiously. Then Tayler gathers the supple leather reins, takes a deep breath, and slowly puts her foot into the stirrup. Jenny secures the rope hooked to Buck's halter.

"Are you okay?"

Nodding, Tayler removes her foot, places one hand on the saddle horn and the other hand on the seat of the saddle.

I'm okay, I can do this, Buck assures himself. *I've talked to the other horses. Everyone learns to ride here. It's my turn.*

Tayler puts her foot in the stirrup and gives Buck a pat. "Okay Buck, this is it. I'm getting on now."

Tayler gently swings her leg up and over Buck's back. She slowly lowers herself on to the suede seat of the saddle. "Whoa. Easy."

"Pick up your other stirrup. I'm going to lead you forward." Jenny lines her shoulder up with Buck's and makes a clicking noise.

Buck spins his right ear back, listening to Tayler's slow and soft words of encouragement.

"Easy, Buck, good boy," coos Tayler.

Buck's left ear points forward, helping to focus on Jenny's attentive stare.

Tayler's on...I'm okay...I can do this. Buck twitches his muzzle against Jenny's pink shirt.

Sure you can, kid. This is your chance to show them what you've got. Matem encourages from his open barn window.

Welcome to Windy Meadows Boot Camp, son. We've all been there. Better horses for it, too! Charley's voice sounds even more authoritative.

What's going on out there. I can't see a thing, Matem says, looking intensely toward the arena. *Buck's so small I need a magnifying glass to see him,* snickers Matem.

I can see his long ears over the rail. Other than that, he's invisible. Twist turns his horseshoe in the sunlight to catch a glimpse of himself.

Ah, a cool place to lay my belly. Ernie scratches up the ground and nestles down.

Lower your voice, you'll break the kid's concentration, he warns. *Silence everyone!*

Jenny's soft click encourages the hesitant colt to move forward. "That's not so bad, is it Buck?" Jenny keeps a close eye on the young horse and his cautious rider. "Still okay, Tayler?"

"Yep." Tayler manages to push out a quick nod and short breath.

I'm okay, too! murmurs Buck, beginning his second lap along the large wooden pen. *Or at least I think I'm okay.* He lifts his head to catch a glimpse of the outside.

Oh, my gosh! screams Twist. *People, my tail has come unbraided.*

Twist flicks the unraveling silvery locks.

Someone, help! It'll get dirty. He rakes his teeth across the wall of the stall. *Horse hair is itchy. I'm itchy!* His skin twitches all over.

Okay, you know what? No one is listening. I'm pushing the alarm. I am officially panicking here. Twist races to each of the stall walls, searching frantically for a person to help.

Don't do it, Twist, insists Ernie with a low growl, moving briskly to Twist's stall.

I can't handle it. Twist positions his hind end to the wall.

Twist, Ernie barks sharply.

BAM! BAM! BAM! Twist plants both hind hoofs on the back wall near the arena. The noise is as loud as a cannon.

Ernie, now in a sprint, barks loudly, scolding Twist.

You've forgotten our girl's on that untrained colt in the arena.

What was that noise? All the commotion has caused Buck to lose his focus. Buck looks to the barn. *Was it the alarm?* Buck's pace quickens.

Jenny senses the change and pulls down on the cotton braided rope. "Easy, Buck."

Tayler weaves her fingers through the black thick mane in front of her, preparing for a quick dismount if Buck spooks.

Why are they shortening my rope? What's happening? Unable to control himself, Buck jumps sideways.

What do I do?

Buck's side jump sends Tayler's knee crashing into the wall. A quick bolt forward drags her leg down the rough wood panel, making a terrible racket.

"Hold tight, Tayler, I can hardly hold him." Jenny leans back, digging her boot heels into the deep sand. "Pull his head up." Her voice raises. "If he gets his head down, he'll throw you."

"I can't. He's got the bit in his teeth." Tayler struggles to tighten the reins.

"He won't turn loose. Come on, Buck, let go," she demands.

NO! Buck springs into the air, his head between his knees and his heels high over Tayler's head.

Oh, boy. Charley grinds his teeth. *Trouble, big trouble,* Charley says, pacing a nervous stall circle. He turns to pin his ears at Twist. *This is your fault, pretty boy.*

Buck's bucking? Matem startles out of another horse show daydream.

Yeah, thanks to Twist kicking his stall wall, Charley yells. *I can't see. There's too much dust.*

Is our girl okay? We need a report, Matem calls out.

Dripping with sweat and with heart racing, Buck jolts to a halt and faces Jenny. Jenny stares into Tayler's wide eyes. "I was sure you were coming off the hard way." Jenny takes the slack out of her rope and gives Tayler's leg a pat.

"You and me both. One more of those rodeo jumps and I would've been a goner." She adjusts her helmet and shifts the saddle back in place.

"Tayler, if you're okay, we'll need to start again. We have to end on a positive note. Jenny, go ahead when you're ready." Miss Ellie points to the rail.

Jenny agrees, nodding her head. "We sure do. Ready, Tayler?"

Ernie? What do I do? Buck trembles.

Buck, you must be brave and focus. Ernie sits patiently at the gate.

I don't know what happened. I heard the alarm and I lost it. Buck leans his head on Jenny's arm. *How do I say, I'm sorry?*

You can't, Buck, you just never, ever do that again, warns Ernie, still overseeing the work from the gate. *There is no room here for naughty horses. You do your best. I have some unfinished business in the barn.* Ernie trots away.

It's over. No big deal. Everyone's fine. Jack Russell trots by, nose in the air, too busy to stop with details.

Ernie marches up to the stall door. *Twist, I'm talking to you. An unbraided tail is not an emergency.*

Twist stands with his tail to the door. *It's my tail. It's very valuable. Not everyone can grow a tail this long and perfect and keep it clean.* Twist sifts the shavings with his nose.

"That's much better. I'll get Buck un–tacked and cooled down. You check Twist and see what happened." Jenny steadies Buck, while Tayler steps to the ground.

"My legs are a little shaky," Tayler laughs, bending down to check her knee.

The three leave the arena and go into the barn. Jenny takes Buck to the wash stall to be unsaddled and rinsed off.

"Hey, Twist." Tayler's familiar voice drifts through the bars. "What happened?"

Twist swishes his thick silver tail back and forth and looks over his shoulder for Tayler's reaction.

Her blue eyes sparkle. "Oh, I see your tail's come unbraided. It's hanging in the shavings getting dirty. I know you hate that. Let me put it up for you. I'll be right back." Tayler crosses the aisle for a rubber band. "Come here, Twist." Tayler motions with her hands and whistles. He doesn't budge. "Twist?"

He turns slowly, looking so ashamed. *I'm sorry Tayler, I didn't mean to scare Buck.*

"It's okay, I'm fine. A little shaky, but good." Tayler reaches for his halter.

Jenny stops at the stall. "What happened?"

Tayler holds up Twist's tail. "It came unbraided." She picks out each piece of sawdust. "He's my most sensitive horse." She pats the top of his massive hindquarters and smiles.

Don't be nice to him, Charley stomps and snorts. *He nearly got you hurt. There's no room for self–centered soldiers in this horse's army! That goes for you too, Buck.* Charley glares at the colt.

"Easy, Charley. I'm almost done with Twist's tail. I will take you for a walk before dinner." Tayler winks and blows Charley a kiss.

Miss Ellie stops by the wash rack. "Hey, Jenny, is Buck okay?"

"Your daughter's quite a cowgirl," Jenny laughs, scraping the extra water from Buck's coat.

"I was scared at first, but then I just calmed down and stayed with him. I just kept saying, 'I'm not going to fall off.' I must admit it was fun." Tayler leads Charley from his stall.

"That kind of fun is bad for your mother's health and maybe yours too." Miss Ellie plants a kiss on Tayler's rosy cheek and gives Charley a pat. Miss Ellie checks her watch. "It's close to feeding time. George and Pam did the watering before they left, so we need to hay and grain."

See, you guys. Tayler thought it was fun. She even said so, Twist stuck his tongue out at Charley.

You should be more careful. Ernie peers up as he passes by.

It all worked out. Tayler is fine, my tails up, and Buck learned his lesson, Twist shrugs.

It all worked out this time, Ernie sighs, *but next time it might be different.*

Dinner. It's almost dinner time, sings Matem. *Hey, hey, it's the hay cart.* The metal tap of the feed doors can once again be heard, as grain is poured into each one along the way.

Corn, oats, corn, oats. Matem zips back and forth in his stall trying to catch a glimpse of the feed cart.

Charley's heavy steps shake the ground.

My walk with Tayler was great. She sat on me bareback while I grazed in the fresh grass. Maybe I should do a little exercise on my way back.

Charley jogs in place next to Tayler. "Wait, Charley, settle down." Tayler yanks the lead down.

Where's that cart? Who has it? Matem calls down the aisle.

I've got it, Bravo answers back, with a mouthful of grain.

I'm being served right now, brags Guess Who. *Yum, Matem you don't know what you're missing.*

Don't tease me like that, Guess Who. I can smell that sweet grain from here.

Matem turns his nose up high in the air. *It's making me drool. I'm always the last one to be fed at night. I'm starving.*

Yes, but you're the first to be fed in the morning, whispers the mouse.

Oh, you again. Matem drops his eyes to the ground. *Looking for a handout? A freebie? There won't be any here. You can move, you know. There are 149 other stalls. Beat it, mouse!*

Oh, but you are the messiest eater on this whole farm and I'm always guaranteed a hearty meal. Waiting to catch a morsel, the mouse eagerly rubs his hands together.

The familiar metal tap and Pete's beet pulp splatters into his bucket. Matem knows he's next.

Hay first, please. The door slides open, as if he cued it. Matem lunges at the green flakes and Miss Ellie puts herself between Matem and his feeder. "I asked you not to grab the hay, you'll bite my hand."

That's right, don't bite the hand that feeds me, Matem laughs. *I just tickle myself.* Then comes his favorite sound, the tap of the metal feeder. *Oh, my grain. Wow, did you just hear that?*

Was that thunder? Or did Twist toot? Sneaky Pete looks up from his bucket.

I don't toot, Twist huffs.

No, it's my stomach. Matem dives face–first into his feeder, briefly coming up for air. *Dinner...the most important meal of the day.*

The hay and grain carts are re–stocked for tomorrow's feeding and the barn is quiet. The sound of munching and crunching is all that is heard.

"Time to go home. We start over tomorrow." Miss Ellie walks the aisle, heading for the parking lot. "Good night, horses."

Last one to the car is a smelly hound. Jack Russell flies by other dogs and out the door.

We are smelly hounds. Ernie picks up the pace and heads out the doors. "I'll get the lights," Tayler calls. "I want to say goodnight."

"Bye, Tayler. Good rides." Jenny waves, as she climbs into her car. "See you tomorrow."

Tayler clicks the aisle lights off. The night lights illuminate, lighting her way down the long aisle. "Good night, Twist. You are the most beautiful horse in the world." She pulls a carrot from her pocket and pokes it through the bars.

Bye, Tayler. Twist adjusts the carrot to get a better grip.

"See you tomorrow, Charley. Soon your foot will be better and we'll get back to work. I miss riding you." Charley rubs his muzzle in the empty feeder. *Carrot, please.* "Sure, Charles." Thump...a carrot appears.

"One of these days, you and I will win the world, Guess Who." Tayler smiles and continues her walk.

I'm counting on it. The pony follows her with his big brown eyes. *Ahem! Aren't you forgetting someone?* Matem whinnies, causing Tayler to burst out laughing. "You are such a ham. Do you want a carrot?"

That's a silly question. No, I don't want a carrot, I want them all.

"Good night, Matem. I love you."

I love you too, Tayler, and carrots. I love carrots. Good night. One final hug and Tayler's gone.

The gates of Windy Meadows swing shut behind the last car. The barn is closed now and will reopen in the morning. You know how to find your way back any time you want to hear more *Tails of Windy Meadows*. Don't be a stranger. Come and see us.

And in the distance, Matem whinnies. *Does anyone have any leftovers? I could use a snack.*

Go to sleep, Matem! The mouse nestles into his bed of shavings and hay. *How long until breakfast?* Matem whispers.

The End

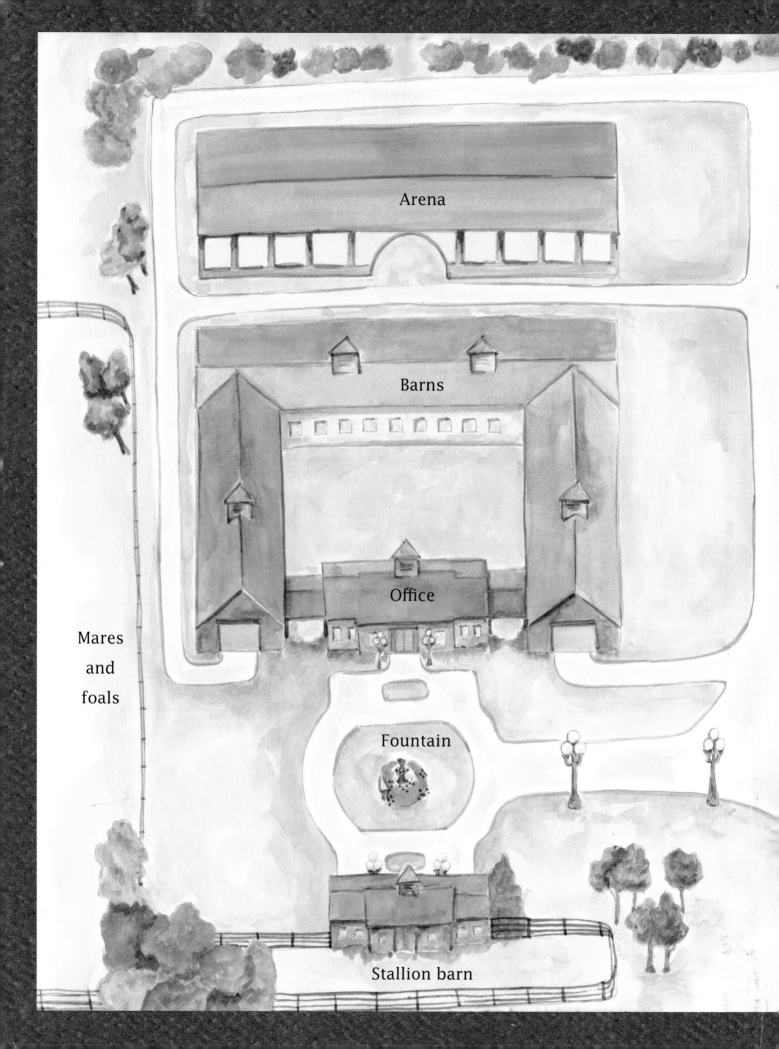